Put Beginning Readers on the Right Track with
ALL ABOARD READING™

The All Aboard Reading series is especially designed for beginning readers. Written by noted authors and illustrated in full color, these are books that children really want to read—books to excite their imagination, expand their interests, make them laugh, and support their feelings. With fiction and nonfiction stories that are high interest and curriculum-related, All Aboard Reading books offer something for every young reader. And with four different reading levels, the All Aboard Reading series lets you choose which books are most appropriate for your children and their growing abilities.

Picture Readers
Picture Readers have super-simple texts, with many nouns appearing as rebus pictures. At the end of each book are 24 flash cards—on one side is a rebus picture; on the other side is the written-out word.

Station Stop 1
Station Stop 1 books are best for children who have just begun to read. Simple words and big type make these early reading experiences more comfortable. Picture clues help children to figure out the words on the page. Lots of repetition throughout the text helps children to predict the next word or phrase—an essential step in developing word recognition.

Station Stop 2
Station Stop 2 books are written specifically for children who are reading with help. Short sentences make it easier for early readers to understand what they are reading. Simple plots and simple dialogue help children with reading comprehension.

Station Stop 3
Station Stop 3 books are perfect for children who are reading alone. With longer text and harder words, these books appeal to children who have mastered basic reading skills. More complex stories captivate children who are ready for more challenging books.

In addition to All Aboard Reading books, look for All Aboard Math Readers™ (fiction stories that teach math concepts children are learning in school); All Aboard Science Readers™ (nonfiction books that explore the most fascinating science topics in age-appropriate language); All Aboard Poetry Readers™ (funny, rhyming poems for readers of all levels); and All Aboard Mystery Readers™ (puzzling tales where children piece together evidence with the characters).

All Aboard for happy reading!

GROSSET & DUNLAP
Published by the Penguin Group
Penguin Group (USA) Inc., 375 Hudson Street, New York, New York 10014, U.S.A.
Penguin Group (Canada), 90 Eglinton Avenue East, Suite 700, Toronto, Ontario, Canada M4P 2Y3
(a division of Pearson Penguin Canada Inc.)
Penguin Books Ltd, 80 Strand, London WC2R 0RL, England
Penguin Ireland, 25 St Stephen's Green, Dublin 2, Ireland (a division of Penguin Books Ltd)
Penguin Group (Australia), 250 Camberwell Road, Camberwell, Victoria 3124, Australia
(a division of Pearson Australia Group Pty Ltd)
Penguin Books India Pvt Ltd, 11 Community Centre, Panchsheel Park, New Delhi - 110 017, India
Penguin Group (NZ), Cnr Airborne and Rosedale Roads, Albany,
Auckland 1310, New Zealand (a division of Pearson New Zealand Ltd)
Penguin Books (South Africa) (Pty) Ltd, 24 Sturdee Avenue, Rosebank, Johannesburg 2196, South Africa

Penguin Books Ltd, Registered Offices: 80 Strand, London WC2R 0RL, England

Digital art by Callaway Animation Studios under the direction of David Kirk in collaboration with
Nelvana Limited. Watch *Miss Spider's Sunny Patch Friends* on Nick Jr., co-produced by
Nelvana Limited and Absolute Pictures Limited in association with Callaway Arts & Entertainment.

ISBN 0-448-44412-7   10 9 8 7 6 5 4 3 2 1

ALL ABOARD READING™

Miss **Spider's** SUNNY PATCH FRIENDS

AFTER SCHOOL RULES

David Kirk

GROSSET & DUNLAP/CALLAWAY

"Ring, ring!" goes the .

The Sunny Patch kids

close their .

 is done for the day.

The is shining.

"Time to play!" says .

The Sunny Patch kids go

to the Dribbly Dell.

There are lots of

and soft  .

And the Sunny Patch

kids love to play

by the  .

"What should we play?"

asks .

and reach

into their .

"I have a soccer- ,"

says 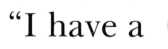.

"I have a -berry,"

says .

8

"I do not want to play

soccer-  ," says  .

"We <u>always</u> play soccer- 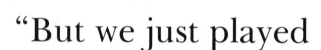 ."

"But we just played

 -berry yesterday,"

says  .

"I do not want to play

 -berry."

"Let's choose blades of ," says .

" , if you pick the shorter blade, we'll play soccer-.

, if you pick the shorter blade, we'll play  -berry."

 picks the shorter blade of .

"Soccer- it is!" says .

"But I do not want

to play soccer-!"

 shouts.

"I want to go home."

"Wait!" says .

"I have an idea."

"We can play soccer-

and -berry,"

says  .

"That way everyone can

play the game they want."

"Great idea!" says  .

"Yay!" says .

Everyone is happy.

The Sunny Patch kids play -berry first.

Dragon throws the -berry into the .

"Way to go!" says .

Then they play soccer-.

 kicks the soccer-

into the .

"That was great!"

cheers 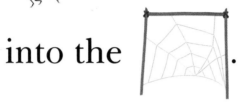.

"Look!" says .

"Mom's here!"
 stands near a

and watches them play.

"Hi, my buggies!" she says.

"It's time for dinner!"

The kids sit at the .

"How was your afternoon?" asks .

"We played two fun games!" says .

"After  <u>rules!</u>" says .

bell	books
school	sun
Wiggle	flowers

grass	water
Shimmer	Spinner
berry	basket

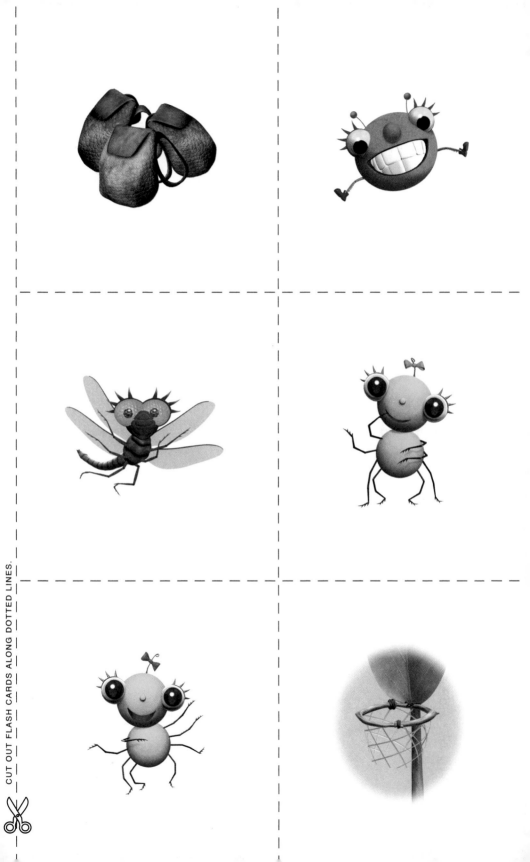

Bounce	backpacks
Snowdrop	Dragon
net	Pansy

Miss Spider	Squirt
tree	goal
table	Holley